LUMAJI

Two Sister Planets Get Another Chance.
But, Will They Learn From Their Past Mistakes

VOLUME 1:
SOLD INTO SILENCE

SERRIAH LE - LUMAJI SERIES
Graphic Novel · Afrofuturist · Fantasy · Sci-fi

For permission requests, please contact:
Serriah Hart
lumajiuniverse@gmail.com
ISBN: 979-8-9925662-0-8
First Edition
Printed in the United States of America

Created, Written, Illustrated, Cover, and
Interior design by Serriah L. Hart

Two sister planets, suddenly bound to the same solar system.

LUMAJI

EARTH

An interstellar conference convenes between Earth's governing body, the Concord Continuum, and the White Lion Extraction Base in Lumaji's Zalkohra Territory to determine whether mineral extraction will proceed under a renewed rights agreement.

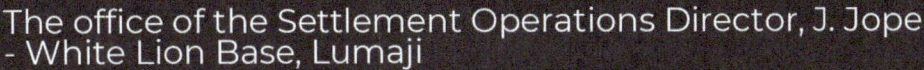

The office of the Settlement Operations Director, J. Jope - White Lion Base, Lumaji

We thought we'd have a word before the briefing.

Sure, come on in.

3

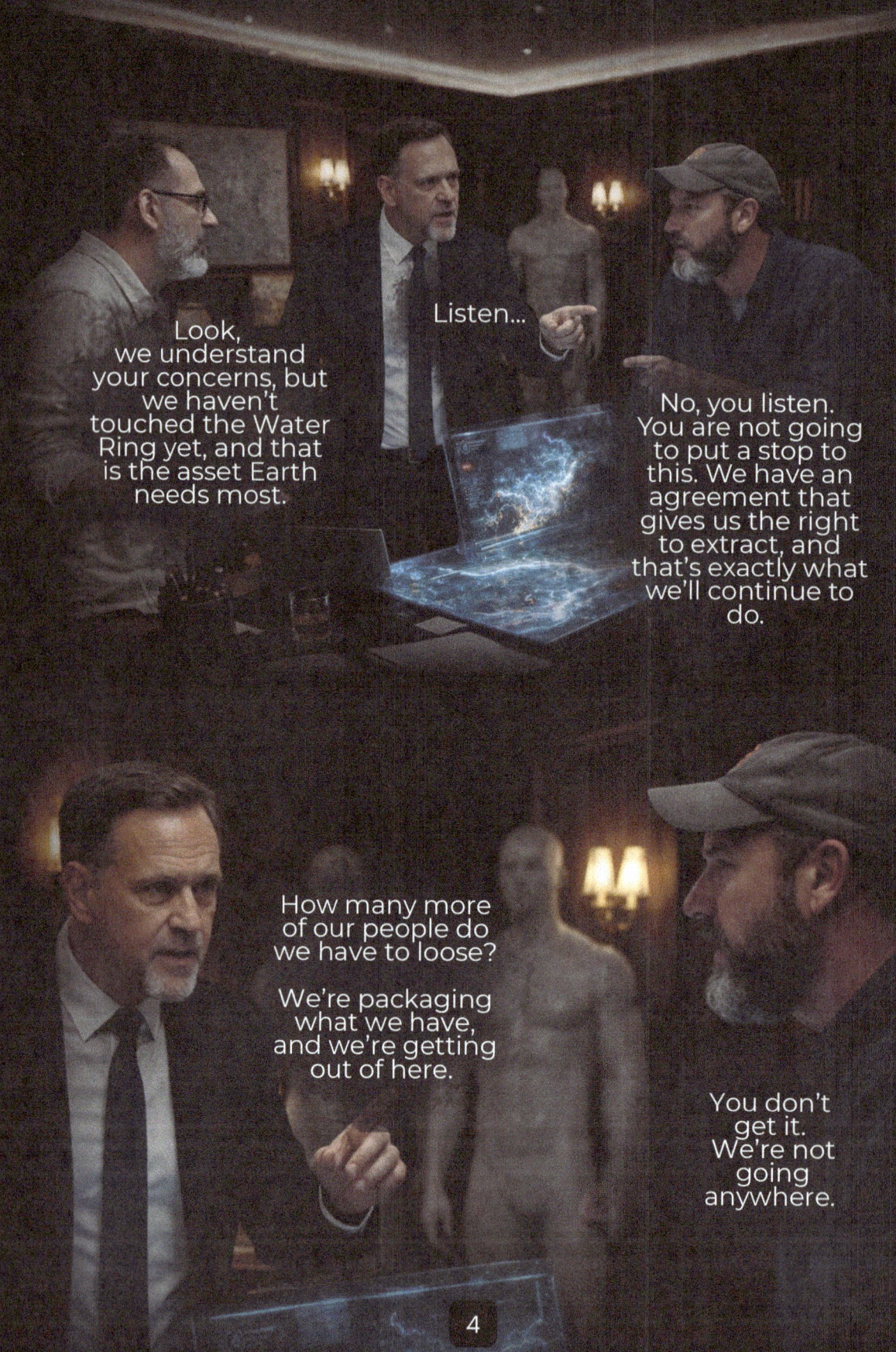

You have no
idea what you're
asking for.
King Bamukwa
is sending his
men to
remove us.
Its time for us to
return home.

I guess we'll
just see what
Commander
Hale has to say
about this.

See you on
the briefing.

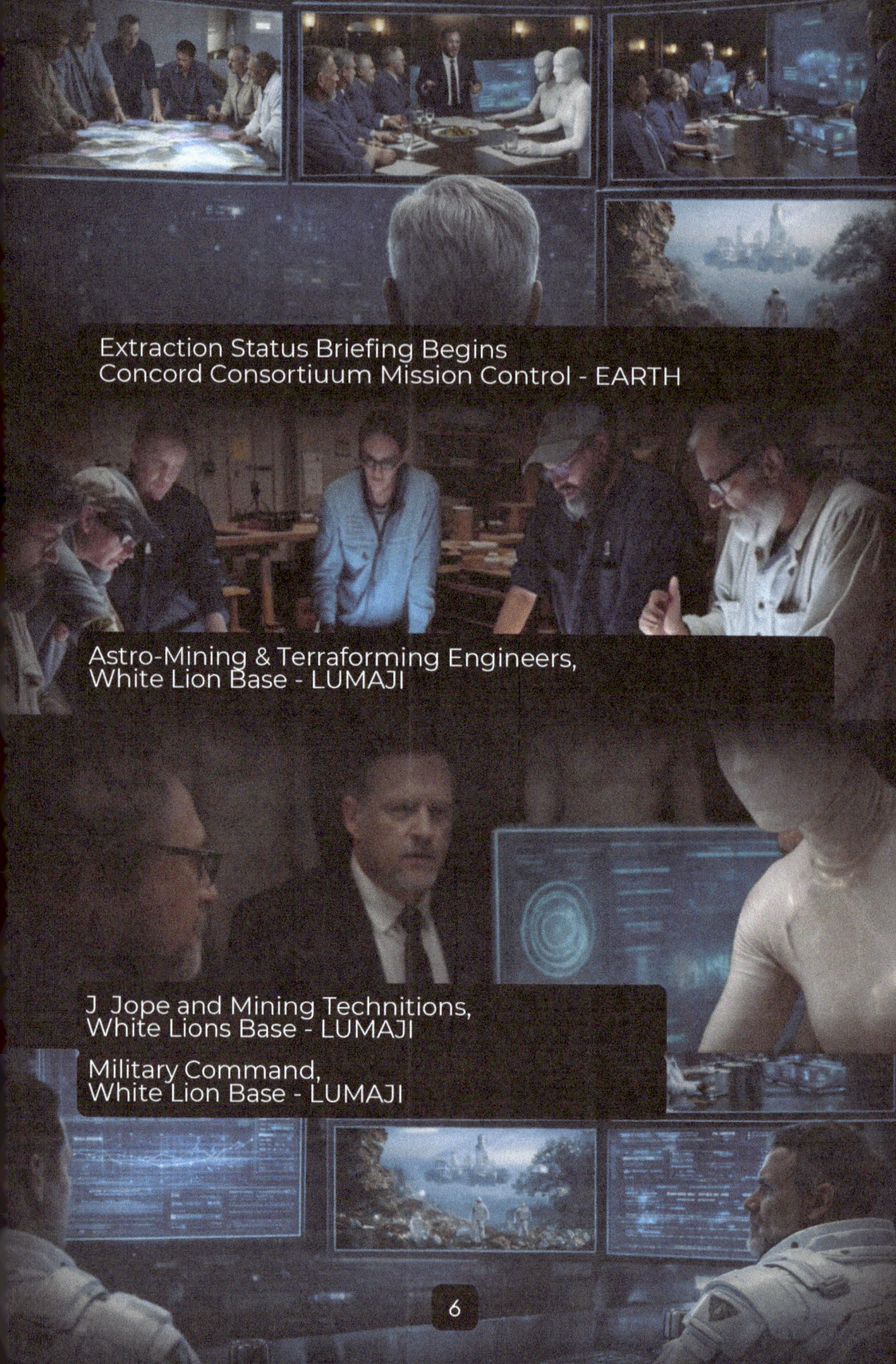

Extraction Status Briefing Begins
Concord Consortiuum Mission Control - EARTH

Astro-Mining & Terraforming Engineers,
White Lion Base - LUMAJI

J Jope and Mining Technitions,
White Lions Base - LUMAJI

Military Command,
White Lion Base - LUMAJI

We're excited to report that mineral yield is far exceeding projections. Enough to stabilize Earth for another 5 decades or more.

7

Let me be clear. We are operating on borrowed time. . This agreement is unstable, at most. They want us gone, and if we continue mining beyond this window, the consequences will be severe. We've already seen what they can do.

In all due respect, I believe Mr. Jope is overreacting. Everything is negotiable. If he's not able to negotiate terms, send someone who is.

All we're saying is, why would we stop now? It's time to EXPAND. There's so much more this world has to offer.

Commander Steven Hale, Secretary of Off-World Operations
- EARTH

Gentlemen, you don't venture into deep space to return with a few barrels.

We will not suspend operations because of their unresolved family conflicts.

Kipulu's Extraction Agreement secures our rights, and Earth will claim what it needs.

We'll reconvene in 3 days to determine the need for expanded militarization.

My men are armed and ready.
You will have our plan in the morning.

J. Jope directs the Mining Technicians.

I don't care what they say! We finish this week, then shut all operations down and get the hell off this toxic rock!

Despite her best efforts, the restrictive bodysuit keeps leading her into clumsy mishaps.

You're new. You'll get used to it once you calm yourself.

But, I can't breath in this thing.

12

14

You know, I've never seen one of you without your mask.

Is it true you people glow?

Let me see.

You'll be alright.

I can even take it off for you.

15

Come on.
Take it off!!!

GET OFF
OF ME!

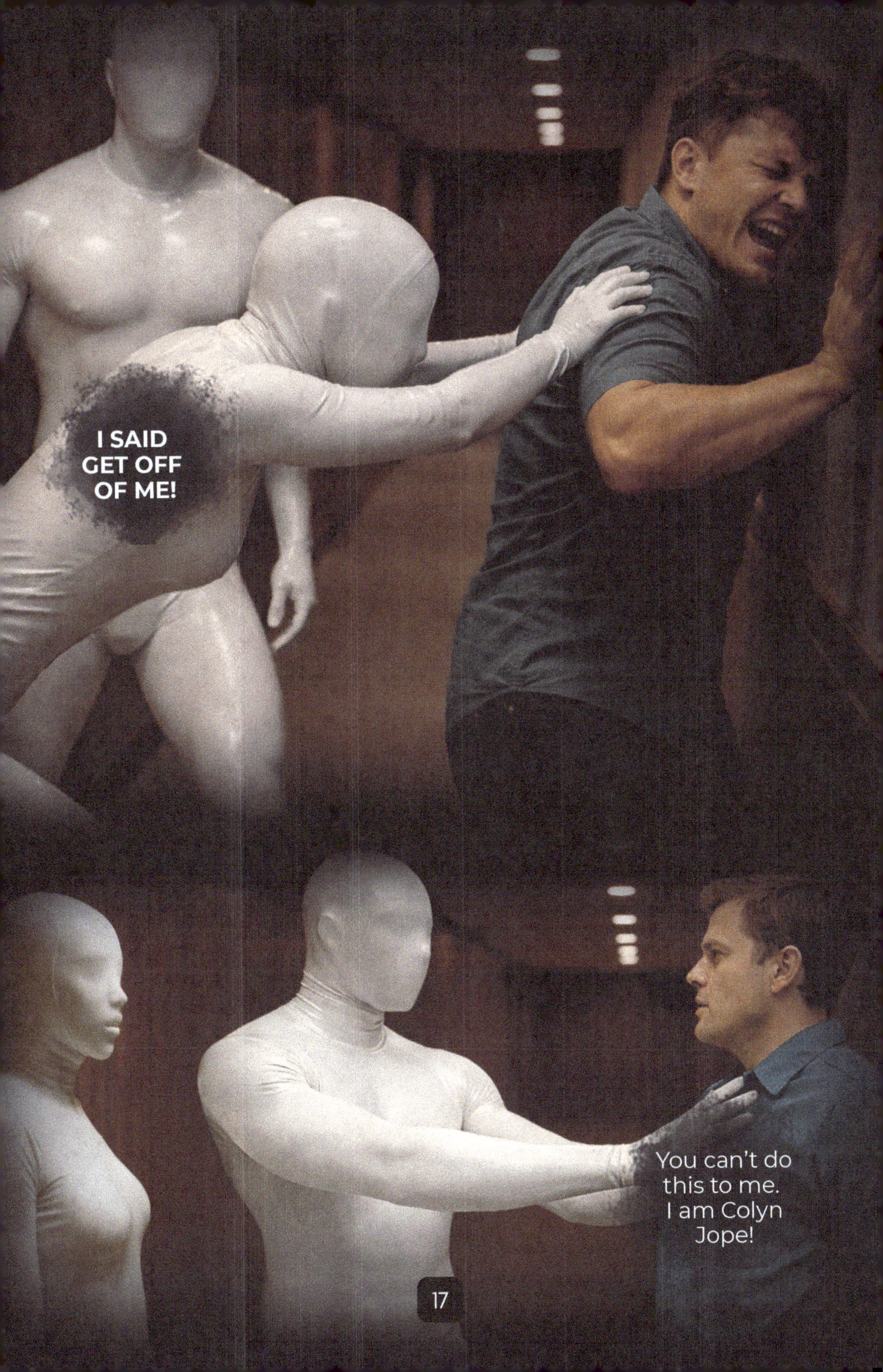
I SAID GET OFF OF ME!
You can't do this to me. I am Colyn Jope!

You're going to have to run.

GUARDS!
Get them!
I've been
attacked!

We're safe now.

I can't thank you enough!

My name is Chivora.

You can call me Velo.

Can we find your home from here?

Yes. I'm from the lowlands. I should be able to make it to my brother and sister.

I got you.

Do you need to rest? It's almost night.

No. I'm good

24

That's it.
That is where
my sister
works.

I see her!

Is this my little sister!!

How!!!

He got me out.

I'll be back in the morning to check on you.

Yes, go ahead. I'll be here to say goodbye to you.

I thought I'd never see you again.

You know, you being here endangers us all. They will come looking for you.

I know, but I had nowhere else to go.

28

Where's
our baby
brother?

He's one of
K'Lier's men
now.

No!

Yes. But, it may work
in your favor.

He'll know
what we should do.
Let me run
and get him.
You stay here, and
I'll be right back.

Alright,
I'll wait.

After much time had passed she begins to realize...
She's been waiting for nothing.

Chivora?

Good morning,
where is your
sister?

I don't
know.

Gone.

She's left me
before.

I should have
known she'd
leave me again.

I don't have anywhere else to go.

You're welcomed to come with me. But, we must leave now, before they come for us.

Is this yours?

Prince, welcome back.

So you're a prince?

Yes, Prince Chimvelo Omilazi of Olindomaji Land.

I know this is confusing, but we have plenty of time for me to explain. For now, get some rest.

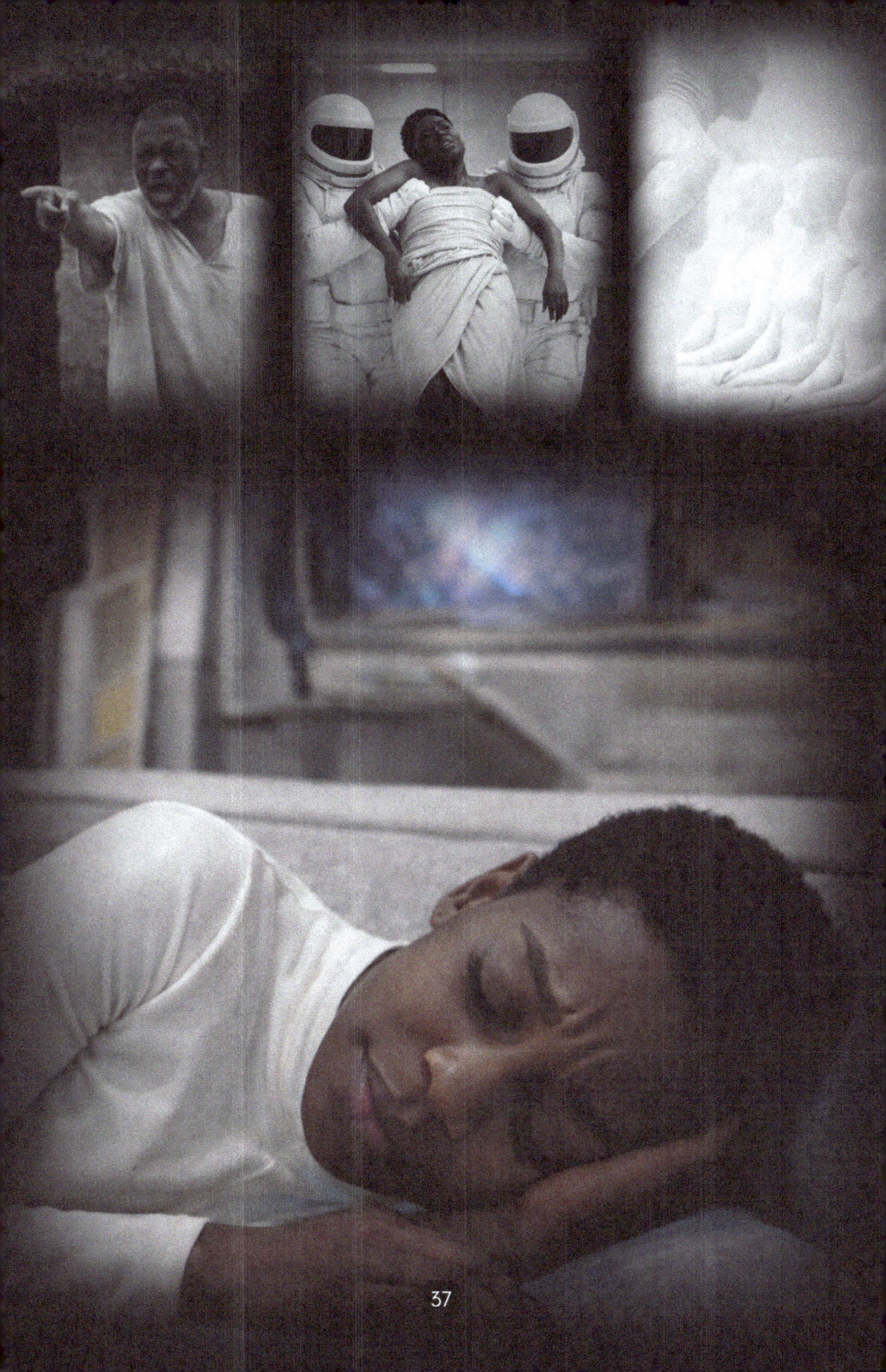

Chivora.

Let me
show you
something

The Water Ring is so clear here. Its beautiful.

I was there
when they
brought
you in.
What led to
your capture?

3 weeks earlier, in her village within the lower banks of the Zalkohra Territory.

It was a normal workday while my brother and I lived with a friend's father, who took us in after our father disappeared. And as usual, he was giving my brother a hard time.

I've had it with him. I want him gone!

This is the last time he threatens to call the Takers on me.

Where are you going? You know he doesn't mean it.

Sis,
I'm sorry.

I'm gonna
hurt him if
I stay.
I have to go.

Everytime you
go missing
you jeopardize
both of us!

We're all we have!

I'll come back for you. I promise.

I still expect you to carry the weight of what you both owe me.

I don't need to know the details, just give me my money.

Blame your father and your brother for leaving you with nothing!

Next thing I knew, I looked up and the Takers were there to drag me off.

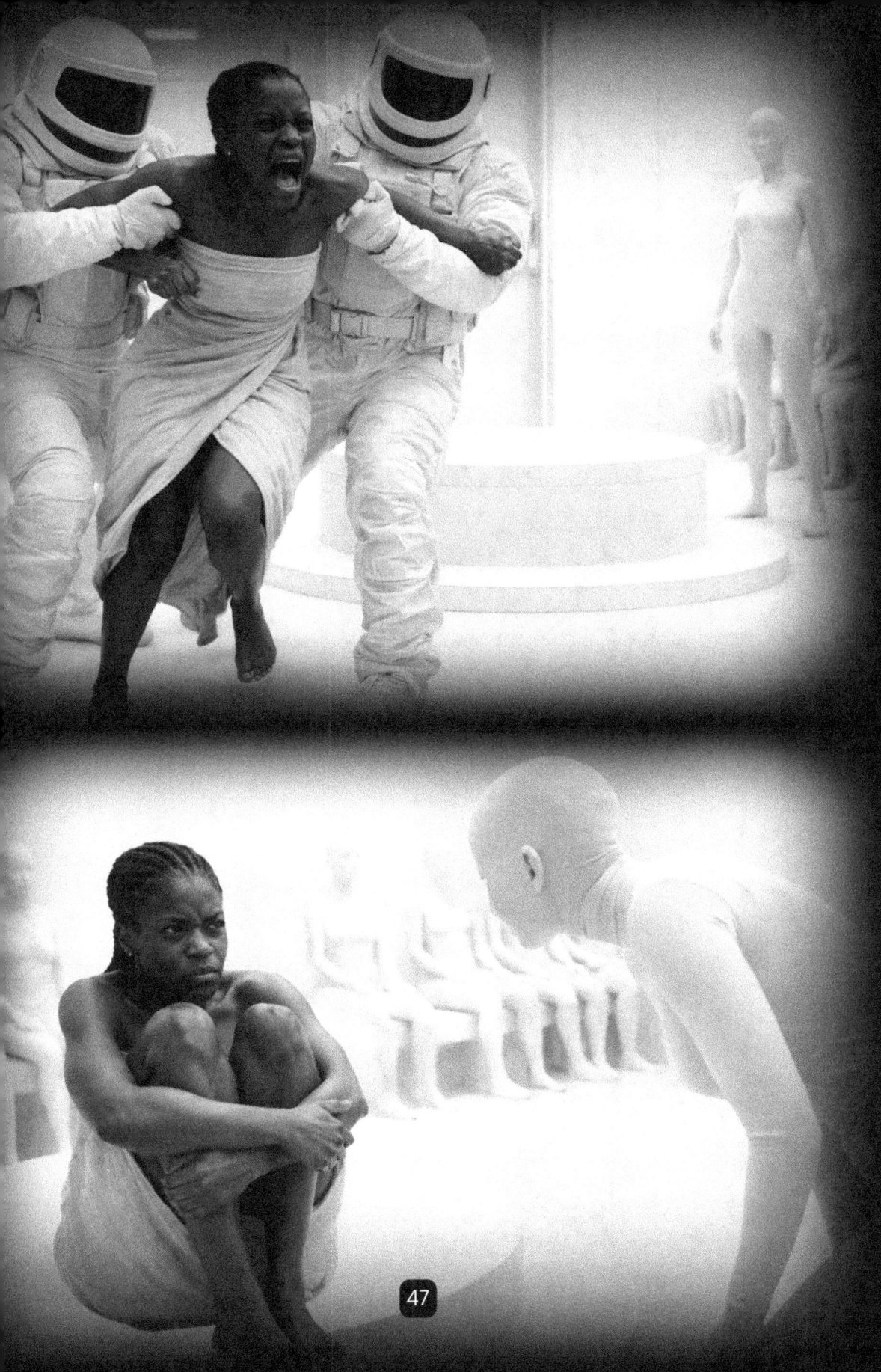

I advise that you keep your suit and mask on at all times. It protects you from the air they breathe and the diseases they carry.

We expect **silence**. We expect **stillness**. We expect you to **watch** and **learn**.

White Lion Asset Sleeping Chamber

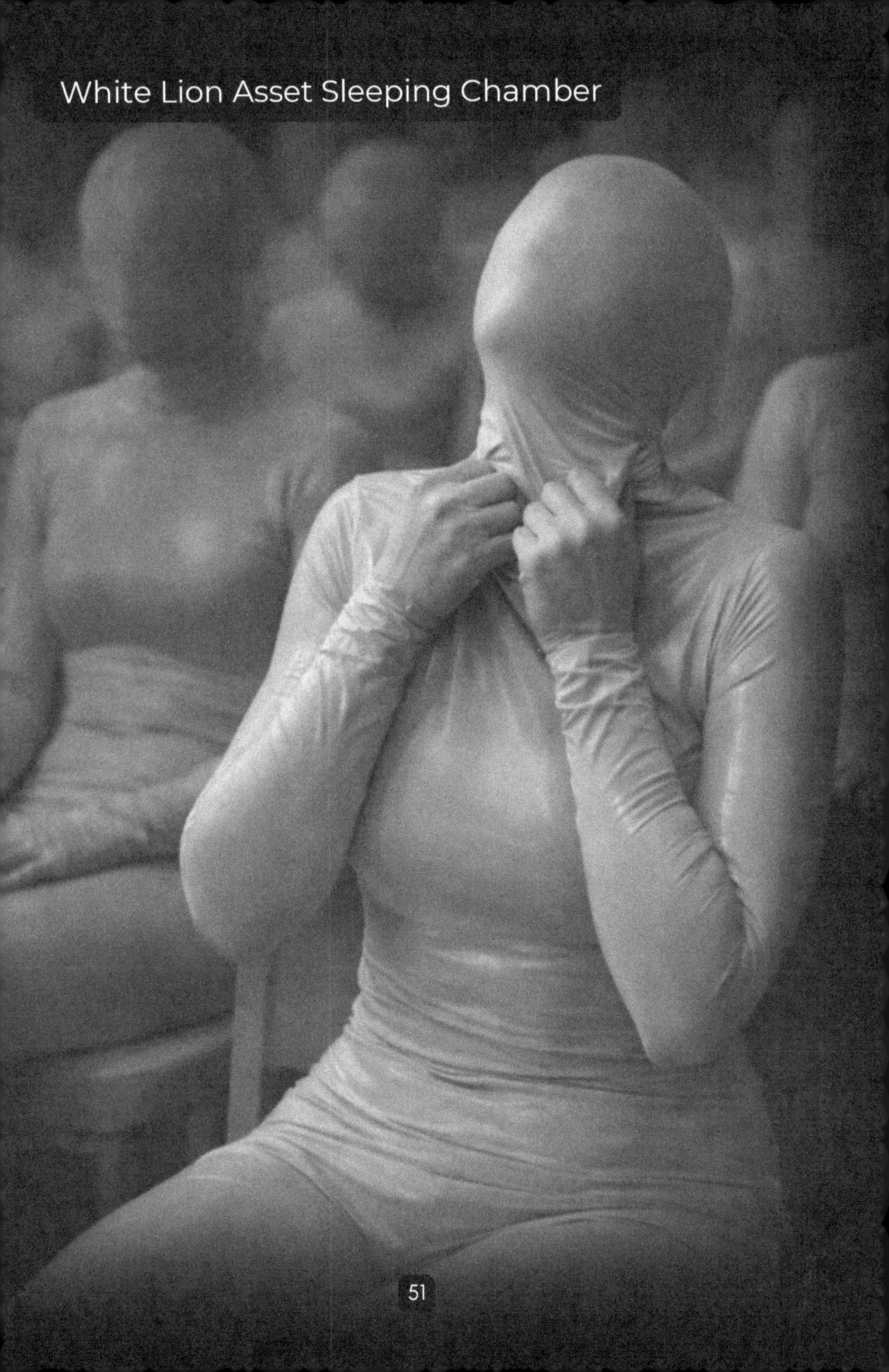

Then it's yours.
tsk... Yeah right.

What about you? How did you end up there?
I walked in.

So, your a Prince, that just walked into the Takers camp?

Are you a spy or something?

Of course.

Something like that. I'm doing what I have to do to protect Lumaji.

And I'm going to need your help in sharing with the King everything that is going on in their camp and the Zalkohra Territory.

What's that over there?

That's my home. Welcome to Nguvu-Maji Coast, the Capital city of Olindomaji Land.

57

Welcome home Prince. Glad to have you back.

Right this way.

Go and tell my father that I need to speak with him in his throne room, Right Now..

Tell the women to prepare a chamber that she stay in.

Just tell the King everything you told me. There's no need to be nervous.

My son is back from saving the world.

And who is this you brought into my throne room?

Her name is Chivora and we both have alot to tell you about...

I allowed you to go,
not because I was
unsure of what I have
to do.
But because I knew
you would return with
what would make the
council confident in
the measures we have
to take.

Be prepared to
present in the
morning, but tonight
we celebrate your
return.

She'll escort you to your chambers, where you can prepare for tonight's celebration.

Don't worry, you're welcomed here and we have everything you need.

Come on
sweetheart,
let's get you
bathed.

This moment of stillness caused a flood of emoitions as Chivora tried to process all that she's just been through.

Calm your mind dear child. Release the grief and fear you've been carrying and let your soul be at peace.

Once sold into silence, she now feels restored, seen, with a sense of resilience that reassures her about her tomorrow.

Meanwhile on Earth.....

The people of Earth who seek survival have begun to migrate to the Population Sustainment Towers, built by the Concord Continuum.

LUMAJI

Unveiling What Has Been Hidden

VOLUME 2: THE TOWERS

SERRIAH LE - LUMAJI SERIES

Graphic Novel · Afrofuturist · Fantasy · Sci-fi